Megan McDonald is the author of the popular series starring Stink's sister, Judy Moody. She says, "Once, while I was visiting a class, the kids chanted, 'Stink! Stink! Stink!' as I entered the room. In that moment, I knew that Stink had to have a book of his own." Stink now has his very own series. Megan McDonald lives in California.

You can find out more about Megan McDonald and her books at **www.meganmcdonald.net**

Peter H. Reynolds is the illustrator of all the Judy Moody and Stink books. He says, "Stink reminds me of myself growing up: dealing with a sister prone to teasing and bossing around – and having to get creative in order to stand tall beside her." Peter H. Reynolds lives in Massachusetts.

You can find out more about Peter H. Reynolds and his art at **www.fablevision.com**

Megan McDonald

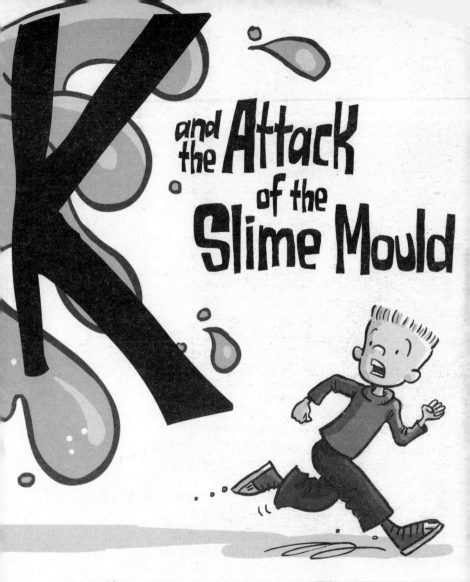

K and the Attack of the Slime Mould

illustrated by

Peter H. Reynolds

WALKER
BOOKS

for Ginger
M. M.

To Jess Brallier
P. H. R.

First published 2016 by Walker Books Ltd
87 Vauxhall Walk, London SE11 5HJ

2 4 6 8 10 9 7 5 3 1

Text © 2016 Megan McDonald
Illustrations © 2016 Peter H. Reynolds

Stink ™. Stink is a registered trademark of
Candlewick Press, Inc, Somerville MA

The right of Megan McDonald and Peter H. Reynolds of to be identified
as author and illustrator respectively of this work has been asserted by them
in accordance with the Copyright, Designs and Patents Act 1988

This book has been typeset in Stone Informal

Printed in Great Britain by Clays Ltd, St Ives plc

British Library Cataloguing in Publication Data:
a catalogue record for this book is available from the British Library

ISBN 978-1-4063-6814-7

www.stinkmoody.com
www.walker.co.uk

CONTENTS

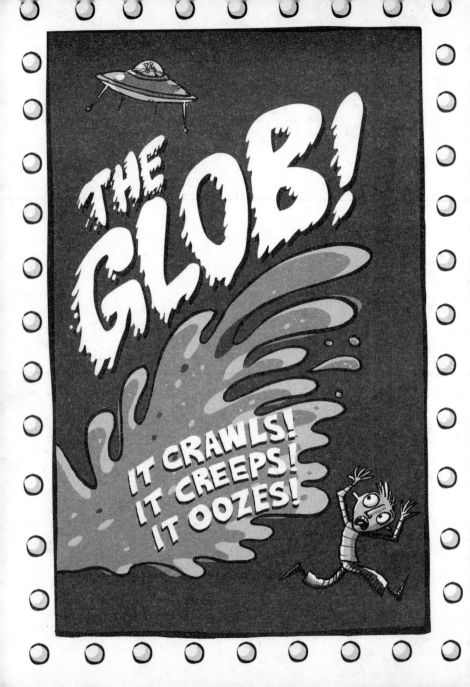

Glip!

Glop!

Gloop!

"It crawls! It creeps! It oozes! It comes from outer space!"

"First it was some sort of blob stuck to his hand. Then it landed on his head. It kept getting bigger and bigger and BIGGER. And then, all of a sudden, he just sort of ... disappeared!"

"What do you mean ... disappeared?"

"The thing ... it ATE him. Right before my eyes."

"Was it a monster?"

"It was worse than a monster. It was THE GLOB!"

"AAAAAGGGHHH!"

"Aaagh!" Stink screamed. He pulled his T-shirt up over his eyes so he would not have to look at the movie screen. Judy jumped. Her popcorn went flying all over the back seat of the car.

In the front seat, Mum and Dad chuckled.

"Whose brainy idea was it to come to the drive-in movies, anyway?" Stink said, with a shiver in his voice.

"Yours," said Mum, Dad and Judy at the same time.

"Well, I thought it would be cool to get to sit in the car and watch a movie. Outside. Under the stars."

STARDUST DRIVE-IN

THE GLOB
AND
SON OF GLOB

5 BUCKS A CARLOAD

SNACK BAR

The Stardust, an old drive-in movie theatre like the kind that had been around when Mum and Dad were kids, had just reopened in Frog Neck Lake.

"It *is* cool," said Judy.

"And dark," said Stink. "And a little scary."

"It's dark at the inside movies too," Judy pointed out. "Besides, it's the Friday Night Freak Fest, Stink. You wanted to see an old monster movie. It's *supposed* to be freaky."

Stink couldn't bear to look at the screen. At the same time, he couldn't bear *not* to look. He peeked out over the top of his T-shirt. A screaming crowd came running out of a diner.

The Glob was oozing down the street.

"It's taking over the whole town!"

"Nothing will stop it, Doctor! It's the most horrible thing I've ever seen!"

Stink screamed again. He turned and looked at Judy with saucer eyes. "What if the Glob eats the whole town?"

"It's not real, Stink, remember? Think of it like a giant glob of jelly. Jelly's not scary, is it?"

Stink leaned in and stuck his head between Mum and Dad. "More popcorn, please." Mum passed the tub back to Stink.

"We're going to have to find the biggest plane we can get our hands on and take this thing to the Arctic, where it'll freeze for good."

"Will that work?"

"We have to do something before it wipes out the whole town."

Stink and Judy watched wide-eyed until the end. "Good thing they found a plane big enough to take the Glob to the North Pole and freeze it," said Stink.

"Poor Santa," said Judy.

"Mum? Dad? Can we stay for the second show?" Stink asked. "It's *Son of Glob*."

"Stink," said Mum, "you covered your eyes for half the movie."

"So?"

"So," said Dad, "I think we've had enough glob for one night. Besides, we have to get you home to bed. Tomorrow you have Saturday Science Club, Stink."

On the way home, Stink could not get the Glob out of his head. When they turned onto Croaker Road, he imagined it following them, oozing down the street, up the path to his front door and into his very own house.

17

That's when he remembered something truly terrifying. He remembered the experiment they were going to be doing tomorrow at Saturday Science Club.

AAAAAGGGHHH!

That night, Stink dreamed of oozy-goozy, blobby-globby goo taking over the earth. When he woke up, he tried to erase it from his mind like chalk from an old blackboard. But even his oatmeal looked like the Attack of the Glob Monster.

All the way to Saturday Science Club, Stink could not stop thinking of globby things. Blobs. Globs. Brains. Oozy-woozy slime. Jiggly-wiggly jelly. When he got to the Discovery Centre, someone was waiting for him outside the front door. That someone was...

Riley Rottenberger.

Sometimes Riley Rottenberger acted rotten. Stink hoped today was not one of those times.

Riley waved a plait at him and grinned, showing off a missing tooth. "Stink! Over here! Are you ready for Slime Mould Saturday?"

"I guess," said Stink.

"You don't sound very excited," said Riley. "What happened? We've been waiting for this since way back when we were doing Weather."

Stink did not want to tell Riley that he was spooked by an old-timey blob movie. So he tried to smile and fake it. "Are you kidding? I'm in. C'mon. Let's get slimed!"

"It's not just slime, Stink. It's slime *mould*."

Riley was already an expert in all things slime mould. Her mum was head of Saturday Science Club. Riley liked to use big words. Stink hoped she was not going to act show-offy all day.

"So what exactly is slime mould, anyway? Animal, vegetable or mineral?"

"No, no and no. Slime mould is not really a plant, and it's not really an animal. It's different from the mould that grows on old bread. Slime mould is a one-celled organism. Kind of like an amoeba."

"But it looks like dog vomit, right?" Stink grinned. "And smells like a corpse flower?"

"It *does* look like dog vomit," said Riley, "but it can also look like brains. Or mucus."

"Sweet!" said Stink. "Anything that looks like mucus is A-OK with me. As long as it doesn't grow as big as the Glob and attack us."

Mrs Rottenberger asked everyone to take a seat. Riley slipped into the chair next to Stink.

Riley's mum drew blobs all over the board. She used big words like *amoeba* and *Protista*. She put pictures of slime moulds on the screen. Some looked like pink spiders' webs. Some looked like red-hot sweets. Some looked like exploding pretzels. They all looked like dog puke.

Stink raised his hand. "So a slime mould is a blob of goo, but it has no brains and no feet?" he asked Riley's mum. "And it can grow and grow and move around like crazy?"

Mrs Rottenberger nodded and said, "That's right. If a slime mould is hungry, it can even join up with other slime moulds. Then they move together like one big sausage."

"A walking sausage. That's a good one," said Stink.

"Has anybody seen the movie *The Glob*?" asked Mrs Rottenberger.

Stink could not believe his ears. He put his hand up.

Riley pulled his arm down. "You did not," she said.

"Yah-huh." Stink waved his hand

again. He practically jumped out of his seat.

"Stink," said Mrs Rottenberger, calling on him.

"I saw it just last night. At the drive-in movie theatre."

"Whoa," said Riley. "Weren't you scared? I was scared of Oogie Boogie, that bogeyman in *The Nightmare Before Christmas*."

"Me?" asked Stink. "No way." He sat up taller and squared his shoulders, trying to look his bravest.

Riley's mum went on. "Did you

know, the idea for the *Glob* movie came from slime moulds?"

It did?

"In real life, some slime moulds can grow to be as big as three feet across."

"And take over the planet," said Stink.

"Only in the movies," said Mrs R., smiling.

Phew.

"Your mum is the coolest," Stink whispered to Riley.

"Look who's talking," said Riley. "Your mum dressed up like a zombie lunch lady once!"

"Oh, yeah," Stink said, sniggering.

"Listen up, everybody," said Mrs Rottenberger. "Today, we are going to grow our own slime mould."

"For real?" asked Stink. "We'll be like Dr Finkelstein, that mad-scientist guy in *The Nightmare Before Christmas*."

Riley shuddered. "He gives me the creeps!"

"Not me," said Stink. "I love how he can pop open his head and scratch his brain when he's thinking."

"Shh," said Riley, pointing to her mum.

"Everybody gets a starter kit," said Mrs R. "I'll help you set up the experiment in class, and then you can take your mould home and watch it grow."

Mrs Rottenberger passed out small glass petri dishes and instructions. Stink could not wait. He tugged on a pair of gloves. He lined the bottom of his small glass dish with a wet paper towel. Then, he oh-so-carefully set the slime-mould sample in the dish. Next, he placed one-two-three oat flakes next to the slime-mould starter.

While Mrs Rottenberger helped the other kids set up their experiments, Stink stared at his dish. He blinked. He watched. He waited. He blinked some more.

Nothing happened.

Stink stuck his hand in the air. "When will it be ready to take over the planet?" he asked. "Or at least my sister's room?"

Everybody cracked up. "I'm afraid it's going to be a while," said Riley's mum.

Stink peered at his tiny blob. "I made you with my own hands," he cackled in a mad-scientist voice *à la* Dr Finkelstein.

"OK, junior scientists," said Mrs R. "When you're ready, put your slime mould dish in a shoe box. Take it home and keep it in a warm, dark place. But not too warm – you don't want it to dry out."

Stink peered down at the petri dish in his shoe box. It was hard to believe that one tiny dab of goo could grow into a giant glob.

"Check on your mould in ten or twelve hours. Write down any changes you notice. Next week we'll be building solar ovens to melt chocolate. We can look over your slime-mould journals again in two weeks. Class is over for today."

"Two weeks?" said Stink. "By then, I could be blob food!"

"I can't believe Science Club is over already," said Riley. "Rats."

"Slime flies when you're having fun," said Stink.

On Sunday, Stink woke up before Mum and Dad. Before Judy. He even woke up before Mouse or Toady or Astro. He did not read his *Big Head Book of Sharks*. He did not draw Stink Frog comics.

He ran over to his wardrobe and pulled out the shoe box so he could check on his slime mould. Ooh. Sick-awesome! The slime mould was growing. The slime mould was pulsing. The slime mould was on the move. It looked like science fiction. It looked like Horta, a stinky blob in Dad's favourite episode of *Star Trek*.

Stink grabbed his notebook. He wrote stuff down just like Captain Kirk in *Star Trek*:

CAPTAIN'S LOG: SLIME DATE 3196.1
1st day of slime tracking.
Gob of goo starting to grow.
Has made contact with oatmeal.
Slimed three oats!

Stink's heart skipped a beat. He had a new pet! Maybe it didn't have fur like Astro or say "Ribbet" like Toady. Maybe it wasn't the sugar glider he'd always wanted, but it was still way cool!

Stink had to give his new pet a name.

CAPTAIN'S LOG: SLIME DATE 3/96.2

~~Googol~~

~~Goosebump~~

~~The Glob Junior~~

~~Jellybelly~~

~~Sluggo~~

Mr McGoo!!   ← YES! THAT'S IT!

Eureka! Stink ran to tell Judy. "Knock, knock," he called.

"Go away. I'm sleeping," said his sister, hiding her book under the covers.

"No, you're not. You're reading mini-mysteries," said Stink.

"I'm trying to solve the mini-mystery of why you're waking me up so early."

"Come see Mr McGoo!" said Stink.

"Mr Mc*Who*?" Judy asked. She crawled out of bed. Stink dragged her over into his room. Judy peered into the glass dish. "Gross. It looks like snot."

"Does *snot*," said Stink. "It looks like

42

the inside of a jellyfish. Or the inside of a brain! Isn't it the coolest?"

"If you say so," said Judy. "Now can I go back to bed?"

Stink showed Mum and Dad. "And in a week or two, it'll look like dog vomit!" Stink told them.

Mum made a face and stuck out her tongue.

"No dog vomit before breakfast, Stink," Dad said, shooing him out of the room.

"Poor McGoo," said Stink. "Nobody gets you like I do."

✶ ✶ ✶

Under Stink's watchful eye, Mr McGoo continued to grow.

CAPTAIN'S LOG: SLIME DATE 3196.4
Mission Possible: Get slime mould
to keep growing.
Fed one Cheerio, one rice puff.
Slime mould in pursuit of Cheerio.
Good call, McGoo!

That gob of goo grew and grew and grew.

CAPTAIN'S LOG: SLIMEDATE 3196.7
Amazing Observation No. 1:
Mr McGoo size of silver dollar.

I ♥

CAPTAIN'S LOG: SLIMEDATE 3196.13
Amazing Observation No. 2:
Mr McGoo size of silver-dollar pancake!

CAPTAIN'S LOG: SLIMEDATE 3196.17
Amazing Observation No. 3:
Mr McGoo almost size of for-real pancake!

At last it was time. Time to share Mr McGoo with the world!

Stink put his slime mould back in the shoe box and took Mr McGoo on a tour of the neighbourhood. He showed Mr McGoo the crack in the pavement that looked like a great white shark. He showed Mr McGoo the rock where a blue-tailed skink sunned itself. He showed Mr McGoo the best mulberry tree for collecting monkey balls – wrinkled fruit that looks like green brains.

"And this," he told Mr McGoo, "is the exact spot where I found a moon rock one time. No lie. Now it's just moon dust, but that's another story."

Stink passed Mrs Soso's house. "Hi, Stink," Mrs Soso called. "What have you got there?"

"My new pet," said Stink. He held out Mr McGoo for Mrs Soso to see.

"Oh! I think I have a new pet growing on some cheese at the back of my fridge," Mrs Soso joked.

"He's a *slime* mould," said Stink. "It's an organism."

"I see," said Mrs Soso, but she did not look like she saw.

At the corner, Stink ran into Missy the dog walker. Missy the person was walking Missy the dog and a puppy named Anya.

"Hi, Missy!" said Stink. "I'm taking my new pet for a walk too. And I don't even need a lead."

Missy the person peered at the blob in the dish. "That's your pet?"

"It's an organism," said Stink.

"Interesting," said Missy. But she did not look interested.

Missy the dog growled. Missy the dog tugged on her lead. Missy the dog stuck out her slobbery pink tongue and tried to lick the petri dish.

Missy the dog wanted to *eat* Stink's new pet. *Yikes!*

Stink held Mr McGoo close. He crossed the street in a hurry, forgetting to wave goodbye. "Don't worry," Stink told Mr McGoo. "I'll protect you from mean old slime-eating dogs."

Stink raced up the street to the pet shop. Hello! It was Take a Picture With Your Pet Day at Fur & Fangs. Stink's lucky day!

Inside, Webster was getting his picture taken with a fat frog that had a big mouth and looked like Pac-Man.

"Hey! A Pac-Man frog!" said Stink. "Did you get a new pet too?"

"It's my cousin's," said Webster. "I don't have a pet, so I'm borrowing Packy for the picture."

Sophie of the Elves was getting a photo taken with her pet hermit crab, Mr Crab Cakes.

"Where's Toady?" asked Webster.

"Where's your guinea pig?" asked Sophie. "Didn't you bring Astro?"

"I brought my *new* pet," Stink told them, grinning.

"New pet!" said Sophie.

"New pet!" said Webster.

Stink held out Mr McGoo proudly. He lifted the lid off the shoe box. "Say hi to Mr McGoo."

Sophie crinkled her forehead and wrinkled her nose. "So your new pet is a ... slug?" she asked.

"So your new pet is a ... bogey?" asked Webster.

"Slime mould," said Stink. "It's an organism."

"Well, it looks like a giant bogey," said Webster. He went to look for his cousin. Sophie scampered off to find a new shell for Mr Crab Cakes.

"Say slime!" said Mrs Birdwistle, the shop's owner. She snapped a picture of Stink and Mr McGoo.

When Stink got home, he taped the photo into his logbook. Stink and McGoo. Together. For ever.

* * *

The next day, Stink took his new pet to school. Things did not go much better.

"I brought my new pet today," Stink told his teacher. "I didn't want to leave him home alone, him being a new pet and all."

"Stink, you know we have rules about pets in our classroom," said Mrs D.

"I know, but he's different. He's super quiet and polite. He's no trouble at all. And he hardly eats anything. You won't even know he's here. I promise."

Mrs D. took one look at Mr McGoo and pointed to the back of the classroom. "Put him at the back by the tarantula. Just for today."

Stink set Mr McGoo at the back next to the guinea pig food, just to be safe.

Mrs D. also let Stink sit at the back of the class for the day. While she talked on about consonant blends,

Stink checked and rechecked his slime mould. All the kids who walked past Mr McGoo said "Yuck" or "Ooh" or "Gross".

"Just ignore them," Riley said to Stink.

CAPTAIN'S LOG: SLIMEDATE 3\96.21
Not everybody appreciates science.
McGoo looking jittery.   ⍩
Check back at 0900 hours.
Expect further difficulty.

"Slime moulds are very scientific," Stink said, trying to convince them.

"Tell them they can solve mazes," said Riley. She nudged Stink with her elbow.

"Slime moulds can solve mazes," said Stink. "Pretty smart for not having a brain, huh?"

"And they can power robots," Riley whispered to Stink.

"And did you know slime moulds can power robots?" Stink said. "No lie."

Webster shrugged. Stink could tell Sophie didn't believe him. The other kids just stared.

"*And* they make good pets because they don't shed all over the place. They don't bark or bite or make loud noises."

But everybody seemed more interested in consonant blends than slime moulds. Even though *slime mould* had not one but TWO consonant blends!

CAPTAIN'S LOG: SLIMEDATE 3196.22
Rough morning at school.
McGoo having trouble making friends.
Does not play well with others.

* * *

At lunch, nobody but Riley Rottenberger wanted to sit next to Stink and his slime mould. At break time, Webster made bogey jokes. And in maths class, Sophie said she was allergic to mould and moved to another desk.

During Not-So-Silent Reading, a kid pointed and said, "Hey! Your science project is getting out of its container."

"He's not my science—"

"He's attacking the guinea pig food," said another kid.

Maybe Mr McGoo was a little bit hungry after all. Stink raised his hand and asked for a hall pass. He went straight to the cafeteria to ask the lunch lady for a Cheerio. He sure could use some cheery-o-ing up. But the lunch lady did not have a Cheerio.

All she had was Raisin Bran. Even a slime mould wouldn't eat boring old Raisin Bran.

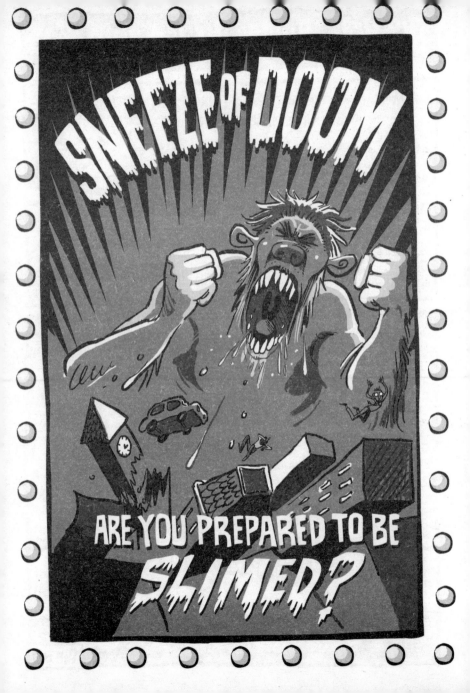

When Stink got home from school, he took Mr McGoo upstairs. Mr McGoo looked a little raisiny – as wrinkled as a monkey ball. "I know you had a bad day at school," Stink said. "But look on the bright side. At least YOU don't have any homework."

CAPTAIN'S LOG: SLIMEDATE 3196.23
Mr McGoo does <u>not</u> like Raisin Bran.
Mr McGoo <u>does</u> look like a raisin.

To cheer him up, Stink told Mr McGoo, "Riley's coming over." Riley Rottenberger could be annoying, for sure, but at least she was a good partner in slime. In baby talk, Stink said, "Riley likes slime mould. Yes, she does."

"Slime time!" Riley said when she got to Stink's house. Stink moved his light-up globe closer so they could inspect their pets. "My slime mould is

way bigger than your slime mould,"
Riley said in a braggy voice.

"Don't listen to her, Mr McGoo,"
whispered Stink.

"I like how you gave your slime
mould a cool name," said Riley.

"Didn't you name yours?" asked
Stink.

"Um," said Riley. "Sure. Its name is ... um ... Mrs McGoo."

"Gross!" said Stink. "Our slime moulds are not married."

"Fine. Then I'll change her name to Princess Slime Mould."

"How did you get Princess Slime Mould to grow so much?" Stink asked.

"Easy cheesy," said Riley. "I fed her. And you have to do stuff that makes her happy. Like they had us do for the animals at that farm we visited on our school trip."

Stink remembered. "Oh, yeah. We read books to the chickens and sang songs to the cows." So Stink and Riley sang "Twinkle, Twinkle, Little Slime" to Mr McGoo and Princess Slime Mould. They read *Squish Squash Moo* till the cows came home.

Stink told a story about the time he got 21,280 jawbreakers in the post *for free*. Stink told a joke. "What do moulds, mucus and big sisters have in common?"

"What?" asked Riley.

"They're all slime," said Stink. He laughed himself silly. "I bet Mr McGoo will grow like crazy now."

"I think you're good to goo," said Riley. "I mean, go." They started into fits of laughter all over again.

CAPTAIN'S LOG: SLIME DATE 3196.26
Attempt made to encourage further growth.
Mr McGoo responds to singing. ♫ ♪
Ruler measurement indicates recent growth
at three centimetres!

"Don't forget to feed him." Riley unzipped her backpack. "I brought snacks!" She held up an apple and a bag of cheese puffs.

Stink took a bite of mealy apple while Riley ripped open the bag of munchy-crunchy cheese puffs. A wonderful waft of cheesy air puffed out of the bag. *Crunch-munch-crunch.*

"Cheese puffs sure are loud," said Stink.

"Yep," said Riley, munching.

"Cheese puffs sure smell milky and creamy," said Stink.

"Yep," said Riley, crunching.

"Cheese puffs sure turn your fingers electric orange," said Stink.

"The better to lick them off," said Riley, sucking the end of each finger.

She reached deep down into the bottom of the bag. As she pulled out a handful of cheese puffs, a small cloud of cheese dust poofed out of the bag.

"A-a-a-CHOO!" Riley sneezed a big sneeze. A giant sneeze. An elephant sneeze! Bits of electric orange gunk flew out of her mouth and landed smack-dab in the middle of Mr McGoo.

Stink's mouth dropped open. He stared at his slime mould. "Gross!" he said. "Look what you did!"

"It's just cheese dust," said Riley. "What's the big deal?"

"You slimed my slime mould!" said Stink.

Riley peered at Mr McGoo. "Stink, you can barely see it."

"You mean that neon-orange Mount Everest in the middle of Mr McGoo?"

"I'm sure it won't hurt him," said Riley.

Stink squinted at her. "Let me see that bag," he said. He peered at the tiny words on the back. "Do you know what's in this stuff?"

Riley shrugged. "Um, cheese?"

Stink shook his head no. "Disodium phosphate, dextrose, artificial flavour, artificial colour, disodium blah-blah, *more* disodium blah-blah. And don't forget corn syrup. Corn syrup sounds good but it is not."

"Sorry, Stink. Cheese dust makes me sneezy. But I'm sure it will be fine."

"Fine? An Unidentified Flying Sneeze just landed on Mr McGoo. It's probably radioactive for all I know. *Anything* could happen now. How do you think the Glob became the Glob? What if Mr McGoo morphs into a glob and takes over the planet?"

"That's only in the movies, Stink. Trust me. It's going to be fine."

"Stop saying 'fine'. It's *not* fine. Sneeze on your own slime mould." Stink could hear his voice coming out like a big meanie. As mean as Oogie Boogie. But he was so mad he didn't care.

"Fine," said Riley. She grabbed her slime mould and stomped down the stairs, leaving behind a trail of cheese dust. It no longer smelled milky and creamy.

It smelled like dog food.

It spelled doom.

CAPTAIN'S LOG: SLIMEDATE 3196.28
Cheese puffs not healthy for slime moulds
and other living things.
Unidentified Flying Object landed
        in path of subject.
Origin UNknown: Riley Rottenberger.
Mr McGoo in possible jeopardy.
        THAT MEANS TROUBLE.

Stink could not sleep three winks. Not two winks. Not one wink.

It was the Glob all over again. Ever since the Cheese Sneeze Incident of 1500 hours, Mr McGoo had been acting strange.

CAPTAIN'S LOG: SLIMEDATE 3196.31
Strange Observation No. 1: McGoo turning odd colour
No. 2: McGoo slimed cheese puff crumb
No. 3: McGoo sent out three new tentacles
No. 4: McGoo crawling out of dish onto
light-up globe

Mr McGoo *was* trying to take over the globe. The world!

Stink tried to sleep, but he kept thinking he felt something slippery and slimy crawling up his leg, his arm, wrapping around his throat. He tried counting sheep, but all he could see behind his eyelids were globs. Slimy, slime-mould globs.

What if his pet had turned into Frankenslime? A freak. A monster!

Stink grabbed his shark sleeping bag by its teeth. He tiptoed out and shut the door to his room behind him. He hightailed it over to Judy's room.

Judy was stretched out on her top bunk, folding gum wrappers to add to her gum-wrapper chain.

"Can I camp out in here tonight?" Stink asked Judy.

"Is it the Glob?" Judy asked. Stink

nodded. "You can have the bottom bunk," she said.

Stink frowned. "It's too close to the ground. Slime mould could climb right up and slime me in my sleep."

"I thought Mr McGoo was your *pet*," said Judy.

"He is. Was. Until Rotten Riley went and sneezed radioactive disodium electric orange cheese dust on him and he morphed into ... Frankenslime."

Stink checked under the bottom bunk. "There's already something green and blobby under the bed!"

"That's just my finger-knitting ball. I used glow-in-the-dark wool."

"OK." Stink climbed onto the bottom bunk and slipped into his sleeping bag for protection.

Judy turned off the overhead light but flicked on her torch pen so she could read.

Stink tried to close his eyes, but they blinked open in the shadowy dark. "Do you hear something?" he asked.

"Nope. But I'd *like* to hear you snoring. Go to sleep, Stink."

"But what if that is the homework-eating sound of Frankenslime? He could be eating my maths problems right now."

"That was just me, turning the pages of my book."

"What if that sound is Frankenslime munching on my smelly sneakers?"

"Trust me, Stink. Nobody would be brave enough to go near those. Not even a Glob monster."

"What if that sound is the munch and crunch of Frankenslime devouring my race-car bed right this very minute? Then when he's done, he comes after me—"

"That was just me, chewing gum."

"Oh."

"It's eleven o'clock," Judy teased. "Do you know where your slime mould is?"

"Not funny. Frankenslime could ooze right across the hall and under your door and..." Stink hopped out of bed.

"Stink! Where are you going?" Judy asked.

He padded down the hall to the bathroom, shining his torch left and right into every dark corner. His heart thumped out of his chest as he passed his room. He tore off the lid of the washing basket, grabbed a T-shirt and raced back to Judy's room.

"Stink? What are you wearing?"

"Dad's T-shirt," said Stink.

"You risked your life so you could wear a sweaty old T-shirt that says 'Minnesota Is for Loons'? You must be loony tunes, Stink."

"Don't you get it? This will disguise my smell. Frankenslime won't know it's me. He'll think it's Dad and leave me alone." Stink got back into bed.

"Hey, why not spray on some of Mum's perfume too, while you're at it?"

"Good idea," said Stink.

"I was joking," said Judy. "Can slime moulds even smell?"

"How should I know?"

"I thought you were some kind of slime-mould expert or something," said Judy.

"Or something," said Stink. He hopped out of bed again and stretched a stuffed snake across the bottom of Judy's door. Then he climbed back into bed. "Do you think it's possible to sleep with one eye open?" he asked.

"Dolphins sleep with one eye open at a time," Judy told him.

Stink closed one eye. He took deep breaths. He counted sheep. Sharks. Skinks. Anything but blobs. Before you could say Frankenslime, his other eye started to close.

Frankenslime made himself as flat as a pancake and oozed under the door of Stink's room. He gurgled and burbled and bubbled his way across the hall. Glip. Glop. Gloop. Frankenslime hungry! Hungry for seven-year-old boy. A thick greenish drool dripped from the corners of the glob monster's slobbery, blobbery mouth. Help! Stink was going to be eaten alive!

Open wide and say...

"AARGH!"

Stink bolted awake from his nightmare. His heart was pounding. His neck was sweating. At least he was alive. *Phew.* He hadn't been Frankenslimed in his sleep.

Stink tiptoed across the hall to his room. He put his ear up to the door.

"Hear anything, Stinkerbell?" asked Judy, coming up behind him.

Stink shook his head no. "You try," he told Judy. She put her ear to the door.

"Hear any slurping sounds? Sucking sounds? Swallowing sounds?"

"Nothing," said Judy. "Slurp factor zero. All quiet on the glob front."

"What if it's quiet because everything in my whole room is eaten?" said Stink. "Poor Toady. And Astro."

"You mean you left your pets in there?" asked Judy.

"Hey, I was busy trying to save *myself*," said Stink.

Judy put her hand on the knob. "You're going to have to go in there sometime," she said.

"Wait." Stink came back wearing a raincoat and wellington boots. He put on goggles. "This is my protective gear." He held the inside of his elbow over his mouth. "I'm going in."

Slowly, Stink opened the door a crack. *Creeeeak!*

"P.U. What's that smell?" Judy asked, waving a hand in front of her nose.

"Told you," said Stink, shutting the door. "My room is slimed. Blobbed. Globbed. That smell is radioactive cheese dust that ballooned up into a mushroom cloud of stink."

"Just open the door, Stink." Judy pinched her nose shut.

Stink opened the door at last.

The room was not slimed. The room was not filled with radioactive cheese dust.

Judy looked around. "I think you're safe, Stink. The awful smell is just boy feet," she said, pointing to Stink's sneakers.

Stink rushed over to Mr McGoo. Something *was* wrong. *Way* wrong.

Mr McGoo looked pale. Mr McGoo looked sickly. Mr McGoo looked like a hundred-year-old shrunken head.

"He looks like a Shrinky Dink!" cried Stink.

"The incredible shrinking slime," said Judy.

Instead of growing by leaps and blobs in a single night, Mr McGoo had shrunk.

CAPTAIN'S LOG: SLIMEDATE 3196.37
Return to SOTC (Scene of the Crime)
Patient in weak state. CAUSE UNKNOWN.
Radioactive cheese puff sneeze suspected.

"Maybe he has Slime Mould Flu or something," said Judy.

"More like Cheesy Puff Flu," said Stink.

"I think Mr McGoo threw up," said Judy.

"He didn't throw up. He just *looks* like throw-up."

"Or maybe the smell of your stinky sneakers finally did him in," said Judy.

"Not funny," said Stink. "This is an emergency."

"Maybe he's hungry. Go back downstairs and bring me three oat flakes and a pancake."

When Stink got back, Judy fed Mr McGoo the three oat flakes. "So what's the pancake for?" Stink asked.

"Me," said Judy, taking a bite. She

set it down on the
what to do. Go to
my doctor kit."

Stink got Judy's way-offi
took out her stethoscope. She   d it
up to Mr McGoo.

"I do not detect a heartbeat," said
Dr Judy.

u hear *anything*?" asked Stink.

"Just you breathing down my neck," said Judy. Next she took Mr McGoo's temperature.

"Is it normal?" asked Stink.

"What's normal for a slime mould?" Judy frowned.

CAPTAIN'S LOG: SLIMEDATE 3196.41
Slime mould reported to sick bay.
Dr Judy Moody taking over command.
Air temperature indoors: 20 degrees.
Slime mould temperature: zero and dropping.
No HEARTBEAT. Keep eye out for
rapid change in temperature.
CONDITION: CRITICAL.

"Stinker. Get me a blanket," said Judy.

Stink pulled the covers off his race-car bed. Judy bundled the blanket all around Mr McGoo's dish like a nest.

"Now get me a lamp."

Stink moved the light-up globe closer.

"Now I need some warm rocks," said Judy. "Pronto."

"Warm rocks? What am I, your errand boy?"

"Do you want Mr McGoo to get better or not?" Judy asked. Stink nodded.

"Then stat!" Judy repeated. "And that, if you don't know, means quick, hurry, now-not-yesterday."

Stink raced outside and collected the first five rocks he saw. "Here. I heated them up under the hot water just in case."

"Perfect," said Judy. She carefully placed the rocks on the blanket nest around Mr McGoo. "We want his environment to be nice and warm so he'll bounce back and make a full recovery.

"Now go get the mister," Judy ordered.

"Mister who?"

"Not Mister who. The mister thingy Dad uses to spray plants."

Stink went downstairs and brought back the mister. Judy spritzed Mr McGoo with a fine mist. "To make sure he doesn't dry out."

"Maybe we should give him some baby aspirin," said Stink.

"Good thinking," said Judy. "I have some in my doctor kit." She took out a tiny plastic container and shook it in front of Stink.

"That's not baby aspirin. Those are Tic Tacs."

"Now get me four pencils," said Judy.

Stink got one-two-three-four pencils.

Judy laid the pencils out on the desk – two up and down and two across, making a tic-tac-toe board.

"Since we have to wait, we can play tic-tac-toe with Tic Tacs. You can be the red Tic Tacs and I'll be green."

"I want to be green."

"Good," said Judy. "Because I secretly wanted to be red."

* * *

After two pancakes each and ten games of Tic Tac tic-tac-toe, Mr McGoo started to look like himself again. "It's working!" said Stink. "You did it. Dr Judy, you could cure a rainy day. Just like Dr McCoy in *Star Trek*. Thanks!"

"I'll send you my bill in the morning," said Dr Judy.

"What's it going to cost me?" asked Stink.

"Let's see. How about one blue-raspberry gobstopper, ten gum wrappers and your fortune-cookie eraser."

"Aw, that's my best one!"

"With a fortune, of course," said Judy. "And you better make it a good one."

Stink knew just what to write.

SOON YOU WILL HAVE THE SLIME OF YOUR LIFE!

McGoo's Log

McGoo's Log — STINKDATE 229.1

HUMANOID ATE BOWL OF CEREAL.
ONLY GAVE ME ONE OAT.
MR STINGY!

McGoo's Log — STINKDATE 229.2

HUMANOID STARING AT ME. HOW RUDE!
HELP — BRIGHT LIGHT!
STOP POKING ME. CUT IT OUT. THAT TICKLES!

McGoo's Log — STINKDATE 229.4

HUMANOID No. 1 MAKING STRANGE
NOISES WITH HUMANOID No. 2.
APPEARS TO BE SOME KIND
OF COMMUNIQUÉ!

No. 2

No. 1

McGoo's Log — STINKDATE 229.6

No. 3

No. 1

TRIED TO MAKE CONTACT WITH
HUMANOID No. 1. NO RESPONSE.

TOO BUSY EATING CHEESE PUFFS
WITH HUMANOID No. 3.

Over the next few days, Mr McGoo grew by lumps and bounds, faster than ever. Warp speed!

Stink built a maze out of cardboard. By the next afternoon, Mr McGoo had slimed his way through the whole entire maze. Stink showed his friends. "Slime moulds find the shortest route through a maze. It's a scientific fact. No lie."

Even Webster and Sophie of the Elves, his anti-slime friends, had to admit it was way cool.

"Good boy," Stink cooed to Mr McGoo. "Who says you don't have a brain?"

"We still think it's weird to talk baby talk to slime," said Webster.

"We still think we'd like your new pet better if it was a sugar glider," said Sophie.

✲ ✲ ✲

Mr McGoo slimed the oat flakes that Stink fed him. He slimed the grains of rice. He slimed the macaroni elbow.

Spores must have landed all over the place, because slime mould was growing on everything. On the desk where sticky maple syrup had dripped from Judy's pancake. Up and down Astro's guinea pig tunnel. On top of Stink's maths book. Mr McGoo had taken over all of Africa on the globe. Not to mention Asia and part of Antarctica.

He even slimed the juice carton Stink left on his desk. One day it looked like a carton of juice. The next day it looked like brains.

CAPTAIN'S LOG: SLIMEDATE 3196.48

Alarming Observation No. 1: SLIME MOULD OUT OF CONTROL!

No. 2: Spores must have spread when Dr Judy misted Mr McGoo. SON OF SLIME!

No. 3: Juice carton left unattended.

No. 4: Mum and Dad found McGoo-slimed juice carton. Violation noted. Action taken.

Mum and Dad did N-O-T want mould growing in the house. They insisted that Stink move Mr McGoo outside. He looked around for just the right spot: somewhere warm and damp with room to grow.

119

The paddling pool!

Perfect. Stink scrubbed out all the yucky leaves and gunk. He set his slime mould in the bottom of the now-clean pool. Next he covered the pool with an old tablecloth, like a blanket. Then Stink wrapped a real blanket around himself, took out his torch, sat in a camping chair and started reading a book to Mr McGoo.

"*All day long he hears squish squash moo...*"

"Stink!" Judy called from the back door. "Dad says you have to come inside now."

"But I'm camping out," said Stink. "I'm having a sleepover with Mr McGoo. I mean, a *slime*over." Stink couldn't help cracking up.

Judy went inside for a minute and came back. "Mum says no sleepover tonight."

"It's a *slime*over," said Stink.

"No slimeover, either. Too cold."

Stink lifted a corner of the tablecloth.

"Night, night. Sleep tight. Don't let the bedbugs bite," he whispered to Mr McGoo. Then Stink headed inside, dragging his blanket behind him.

Stink called Riley and told her all about the Juice Carton Incident of 1500 hours. He told her all about having to keep Mr McGoo outside, and he told her that he wasn't allowed to have a slimeover.

"Don't worry," Riley said. "Tons of slime moulds grow outside. Hey, you want to build a slime house tomorrow? You know, like a dog house, but for slime."

"A dog-vomit house," said Stink, cracking himself up. "Cool! But you have to promise, no cheese-sneezing."

"Cross my heart and hope to slime," said Riley.

Upstairs in his room, Stink curled up in the window seat and gazed out at Mr McGoo until he fell asleep.

* * *

Brring! Ding-ding-ding! Stink woke up. What was that noise? Doorbell! He peeked out the window to see who was at the front door.

Riley Rottenberger!

Stink opened the door. "What are you doing here?"

Riley pointed to Stink's sticky-up hair. "Ha ha! Bed head!"

"What time is it, anyway?" asked Stink.

"Time to start building a slime house!" said Riley, holding up a pink hammer.

Slime house? Mr McGoo! Stink had almost forgotten about him! He ran out to the paddling pool in his pyjamas and bare feet. Riley hurried after him.

Holy elbow macaroni!

There was no tablecloth over the paddling pool any more! Stink peered inside.

No. Way. No. How. Mr McGoo was G-O-N-E *gone*.

Stink turned to Riley in a panic. "Where could he be? He was right here. I put him here myself. I covered him with a tablecloth to stay warm."

"Slime moulds can crawl, you know," said Riley. "Maybe he got lonely and joined up with some other slime moulds and they all crawled away like one big slime sausage."

Stink looked under the deck. He looked beneath the old swing set. He looked in the sandpit. Mr McGoo was nowhere to be found. The slime sausage was nowhere...

"What if Bigfoot came through here last night and thought Mr McGoo was peanut butter ... and ate him?" Riley rolled her eyes.

"Or what if aliens landed in the back garden and thought he was an alien life-form and took him back to outer space?" Riley rolled her eyes again.

"*Or*, what if a meteorite fell on him and—"

"Get real, Stink," said Riley. All of a sudden Riley pointed up at a tree. In the branches. A tablecloth!

"Or," she said, "what if the wind blew off the tablecloth, Mr McGoo got too cold and he shrivelled up to nothing and disappeared?"

"That too," said Stink with a sigh.

CAPTAIN'S LOG: SLIMEDATE 3196.52
UNBELIEVABLE OBSERVATION No. 1:
    MR McGOO GONE FOR REAL!

No. 2: seems impossible but there it is.
No. 3: Stink and Riley mourn his passing.

Stink felt sad. Like the time he buried his goldfish under the rose bush. And the time his millipede croaked. This time around, he couldn't even have a slime-mould funeral.

"Mr McGoo was the best," said Stink.

"He was the best dog vomit around," Riley agreed.

"Remember when Mrs Soso thought he was refrigerator mould?"

"No," said Riley.

"Remember when Missy the dog almost ate him?"

"Nope," said Riley.

"Remember when I got scared and thought he was Frankenslime?"

"Nuh-uh," said Riley. "Sorry. Wasn't there."

"Remember when we read to him and sang 'Twinkle, Twinkle, Little Slime'?"

"That I remember!" said Riley.

"We should have a moment of silence," said Stink.

Stink and Riley stood silently, gazing at the paddling pool, remembering for a moment all the fun times they'd had with Mr McGoo.

"You could always grow another

slime mould," said Riley.

Stink shook his head. "It wouldn't be the same."

"You can come to my house to visit Princess Slime Mould anytime," said Riley.

"Thanks," said Stink. "Can you help me put the pool back in the shed?"

"Sure," said Riley. They each grabbed an end and dragged it across the lawn to the tool shed.

"Want to stay for pancakes?" asked Stink. "My dad makes killer silver-dollar pancakes. Mr McGoo loved them."

"Why not?" asked Riley.

On the way back inside, Stink noticed something about the grass where the paddling pool had been. "Hey, look! I think maybe it's a crop circle! Or a fairy ring! Wait till I tell Sophie of the Elves!"

"The grass is just smooshed from where the paddling pool was sitting," said Riley.

"I don't know," said Stink, looking a little closer.

"What's this?" he asked, pointing to a jelly-like lump of goo in the grass.

Riley took a look. "Is it an ... organism?"

"An organism from outer space!" said Stink.

"Outer-space slime!" said Riley.

"No, wait," said Stink. "I bet it's a silver-dollar pancake ... from Mars! A Martian pancake!"

"That's no pancake, Stink. Not even Martians would eat that," said Riley. "It looks more like an inside-out frog. Frog guts! Cool!"

"It's too big for frog guts. Maybe it's the guts of a *giant* amphibian, like some prehistoric tetrapod or something."

Stink studied the new goo some more. It looked like ... an alien bogey. It looked like an alien jellyfish. It looked like...

Wait just an outer-space second! Stink had an idea. Might it be, *could* it be? Now he knelt down, leaned over and took a super sniff with his super sniffer. The goo smelled like rotten eggs, all right. *Eureka!*

"I think I know what it is," said Stink in awe. He could barely breathe the words. "I think it's star jelly."

"Star jelly?" whispered Riley.

"Star jelly is like a blob of slime

that's left after a meteor shower," said Stink. "It's way rare."

"Really?" asked Riley.

"No lie," said Stink. "Just think. Alien star jelly right here in my very own back garden."

"Wow," said Riley in a hushed voice.

Stink put his face right up to the new blob of goo.

"Riley," he said. "Say hello to Mr McGoo Two!"

10 Things You May Not Know About Megan McDonald

10. The first story Megan ever got published (in the fifth grade) was about a pencil sharpener.

9. She read the biography of Virginia Dare so many times at her school library that the librarian had to ask her to give somebody else a chance.

8. She had to be a boring-old pilgrim every year for Halloween because she has four older sisters, who kept passing their pilgrim costumes down to her.

7. Her favourite board game is the Game of Life.

6. She is a member of the Ice-Cream-for-Life Club at Screamin' Mimi's in her hometown of Sebastopol, California.

5. She has a Band-Aid collection to rival Judy Moody's, including bacon-scented Band-Aids.

4. She owns a jawbreaker that is bigger than a baseball, which she will never, ever eat.

3. Like Stink, she had a pet newt that slipped down the drain when she was his age.

2. She often starts a book by scribbling on a napkin.

1. And the number-one thing you may not know about Megan McDonald is: she was once the opening act for the World's Biggest Cupcake!

10 Things You May Not Know About Peter H. Reynolds

10. He has a twin brother, Paul. Paul was born first, fourteen minutes before Peter decided to arrive.

9. Peter is part owner of a children's book and toy shop called the Blue Bunny in the Massachusetts town where he lives.

8. He's vertically challenged (aka short!).

7. His mother is from England; his father is from Argentina.

6. He made his first animated film while he was in high school.

5. He sometimes paints with tea instead of water – whatever's handy!

4. He keeps a sketch pad and pen on his bedside table. That way, if an idea hits him in the middle of the night, he can jot it down immediately.

3. His favourite candy is a tie between peanut-butter cups and chocolate-covered raisins (same as Megan McDonald!).

2. One of his favourite books growing up was *The Tall Book of Make-Believe* by Jane Werner, illustrated by Garth Williams.

1. And the number-one thing you may not know about Peter H. Reynolds is: he shares a birthday with James Madison, Stink's favourite president!

Collect all the Stink books!

Think you know Stink?

Stink-o-pedia:
Super Stink-y Stuff
From A to Zzzzz

Stink-o-pedia 2:
More Stink-y Stuff
From A to Z

Judy and Stink are starring together!

In full colour!

Then try these!

has e!

www.stinkmoody.com

Go online to:

- Access exclusive top secret content.

- Throw a big Stink birthday bash!

- Make your own comics.

- Learn more about slime mould!

- Read passages that never made it into the final books.

- Find lots of Stink-y information and activities!